Contents

A world of tongues

Earth has a huge variety of animals of different types, shapes, sizes and colours. Most animals, including birds, mammals, fish and reptiles, have a tongue. Animals that don't have a tongue include sea stars and crabs.

All snakes, such as this brown-spotted pit viper, have a forked tongue.

Animal TONGUES

Tim Harris

www.waylandbooks.co.uk

First published in Great Britain in 2019 by Wayland

HB ISBN: 978 1 5263 1216 7
PB ISBN: 978 1 5263 1217 4

Printed and bound in Dubai

Editor: Amy Pimperton
Design: Emma DeBanks
Picture research: Rachelle Morris (Nature Picture Library), Diana Morris

Picture credits:
Dreamstime: Rinus Baak 10br; Lukas Gojda 17tl; Sharon Jones front cover br, back cover tr; Juen-ven Shih front cover tl, back cover bl; Ludmila Smite 37br; Wrangel 21tl.
FLPA: Emanuele Biggi 12b.
Nature PL: Ingo Arndt 17bl; Jane Burton 21bl; John Cancalosi 35br; Mark Carwardine 41bl; Philippe Clément 9cl; Murray Cooper 43b; Guy Edwardes 2, 13cr; Paul Ensor 15tl; Suzi Eszterhas 29tr; Daniel Heuclin 18; Lisa Hofner front cover bl; Mitsuhiko Imamori 42r; Heidi & Hans-Juergen Koch 9bl; Will Burrand-Lucas 26t; Pete Oxford 8, 22; Doug Perrine 14r; Fiona Rogers 38t; Andy Rouse 23bl; José B Ruiz 40–41c; Cyril Ruoso 45br; Roland Seitre 43t; Anup Shah 16; Kim Taylor 10¬–11, 12r, 39cr; Robert Thompson 4r; Andy Trowbridge 23tl; Andrew Walmsey 24; Petra Wenger 34; Wild Wonders of Europe/Widstrand 28b.
Science Photo Library: Natural History Museum 42bl.
Shutterstock: apple2499 20r; belizar 9tr; Bildagentur Zoonar GmbH 4cl; Jarrod Calati 45tr; Mark Caunt 23cr; Comel Constantin front cover tr; Coulanges 42bc; Chase Dekker 41cr; EcoPrint 7bl; FJAH 11cr; Todorean-Gabriel 31bl; Ray Hennessy 19bl; David W Hughes 7cl; Abhishek Jadwani 30; Rosa Jay 37tl; Kletr 25c; Ladyphoto 5tr, 33c; Abdulroheem Lungleengo 19c, 45 cl; MaraZe 7tr; Simonas meyblume 32-33; Minkevicius 17tr; Ulrich Missbach 19br; Omariam 39bl; Matthew Orselli 5tl,44; PhototechCZ 20bc; Andrey Popov 5bl; OndreyProsicky 35tl; reptiles4all 27, 28–29c,40b,46t; Robynrg 31tr; Damian Ryszawy 39tl, 46bl; Petr Salinger 13bl; schankz 36, 46br; Tarpam 14bc; John Tunney 15bl; UniquePhotoArts 3, 38b; Sergey Uryadnikov 26b; Pali VeGa 6; Li Wa 25tl; WilleeCole Photography 29bl.

With thanks to the Nature Picture Library

Wayland, an imprint of
Hachette Children's Group
Part of Hodder and Stoughton
Carmelite House
50 Victoria Embankment
London EC4Y 0DZ

An Hachette UK Company

Northern giraffe

Blue-tongued skink

All sorts!

Just as the animal kingdom is rich in variety, so too are the tongues of the world! Snakes have a long, forked tongue, which they flick in the air, and dogs have a broad one that often hangs from their mouth. Lots of animals have pink tongues, but giraffes have a purple one and some reptiles have an amazing bright blue tongue.

Many uses

A tongue is a muscular organ in the mouth. Our tongue helps us to taste food, then guide it down our throat after we've chewed it. It also helps us to speak.

Other animals use their tongues for many different things. Some of them might surprise you, including tongues for catching prey, tricking other animals and scaring away enemies. Read on to find out more.

Human

Tongues for drinking

All animals need water to stay alive and many use their tongue to help them to drink. If you have a pet you will know the lapping sound that it makes when it is drinking from a bowl. People used to think that dogs and cats drank in the same way, but scientists now know that isn't true.

A domestic cat will poke its tongue in and out of its mouth up to four times a second when lapping up water.

Scoop

When a dog is thirsty, it dips its tongue into the water, bends the tip into the shape of a scoop, or cup, and lifts the water into its mouth.

Beagle

Bengal tiger

Water column

Cats, on the other hand, have a different way of satisfying their thirst. A drinking cat touches the tip of its tongue to the surface of the water, then quickly draws it up. The rapidly moving tongue pulls a small column of water into the air, which the cat catches in its mouth. From small house cats to giant tigers, all cats drink this way.

African lion

Lions like to drink water every day, but they can survive for up to five days without water.

Long, thin tongues

Giant anteaters eat ants, ants and more ants! Relative to body length, a giant anteater has one of the longest tongues of any mammal: the animal is 2 metres long and its tongue is 60 centimetres long; almost a third of its body length!

Papillae

The tongue is covered in tiny backward-pointing spines called papillae and thick, sticky saliva. This speedy eater can flick its tongue in and out of an ants' nest up to 160 times a minute, which is useful when you need to eat up to 30,000 ants in a day.

Strong muscles flick a giant anteater's tongue inside the nest to pull the insects out.

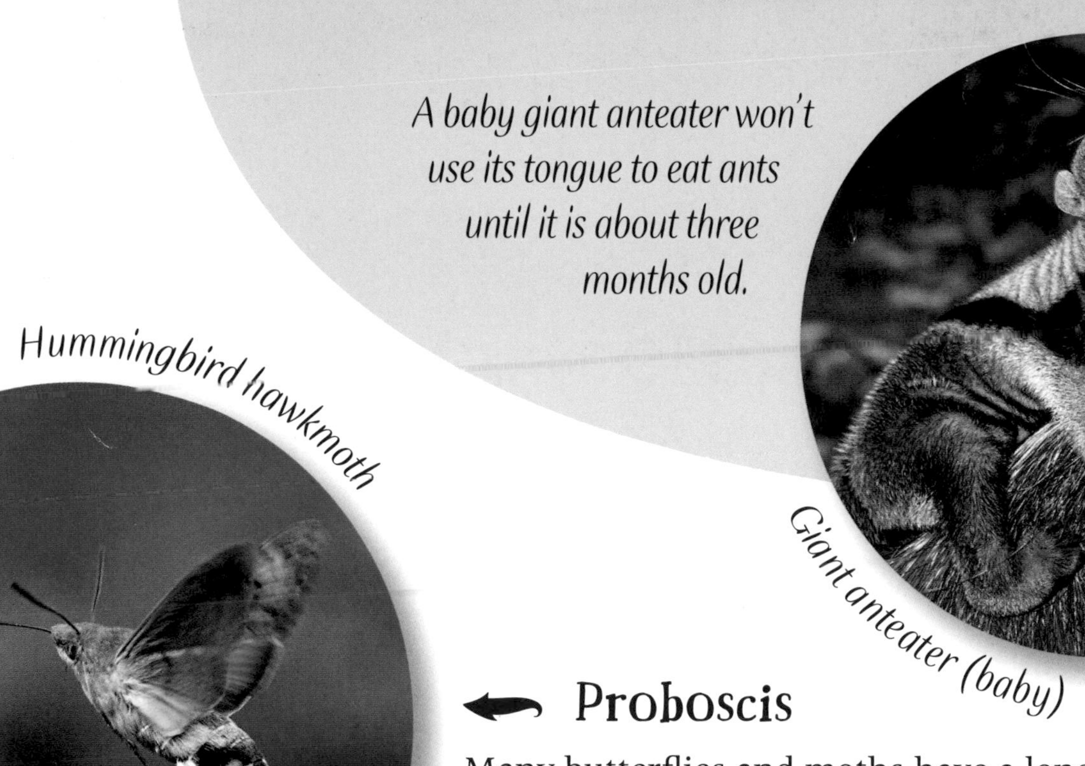

A baby giant anteater won't use its tongue to eat ants until it is about three months old.

Hummingbird hawkmoth

Giant anteater (baby)

Proboscis

Many butterflies and moths have a long, thin, tongue-like organ called a proboscis. This hollow tube is used to suck a sugary liquid called nectar from flowers. Usually, it is tightly coiled under the insect's head, but it is unwound to suck the energy-giving nectar. Some moths have a tongue that is longer than their body! (See page 42.)

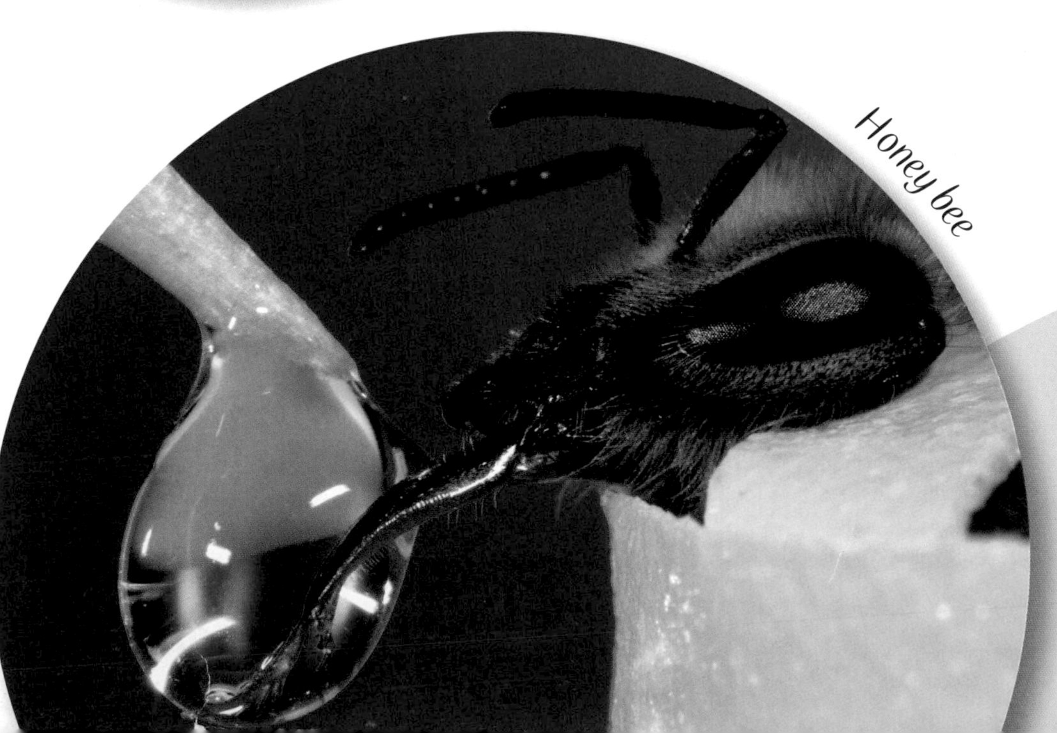

Honey bee

A honey bee sucks up nectar through its straw-like proboscis.

Tongues for striking

Although chameleons are best known for being able to change colour, these tropical reptiles are also amazing for their all-action tongues, which act like sticky darts.

A chameleon's tongue is as long or even longer than its body. When a chameleon sees insect prey within range, it shoots out its tongue at incredible speed (see pages 40–41). These reptiles don't believe in eating slowly: the whole operation takes as little as 0.07 seconds!

The blunt tip of the tongue is sticky. It attaches to the insect and pulls it back into the chameleon's mouth.

Mechanical pulling

Unlike most animals, a frog's tongue is attached to the front of its lower jaw and folded up inside the mouth. When a frog's next meal comes close enough, the frog flips its tongue out of its mouth to strike the prey and then pulls the prey back into its mouth. This tongue motion is called mechanical pulling.

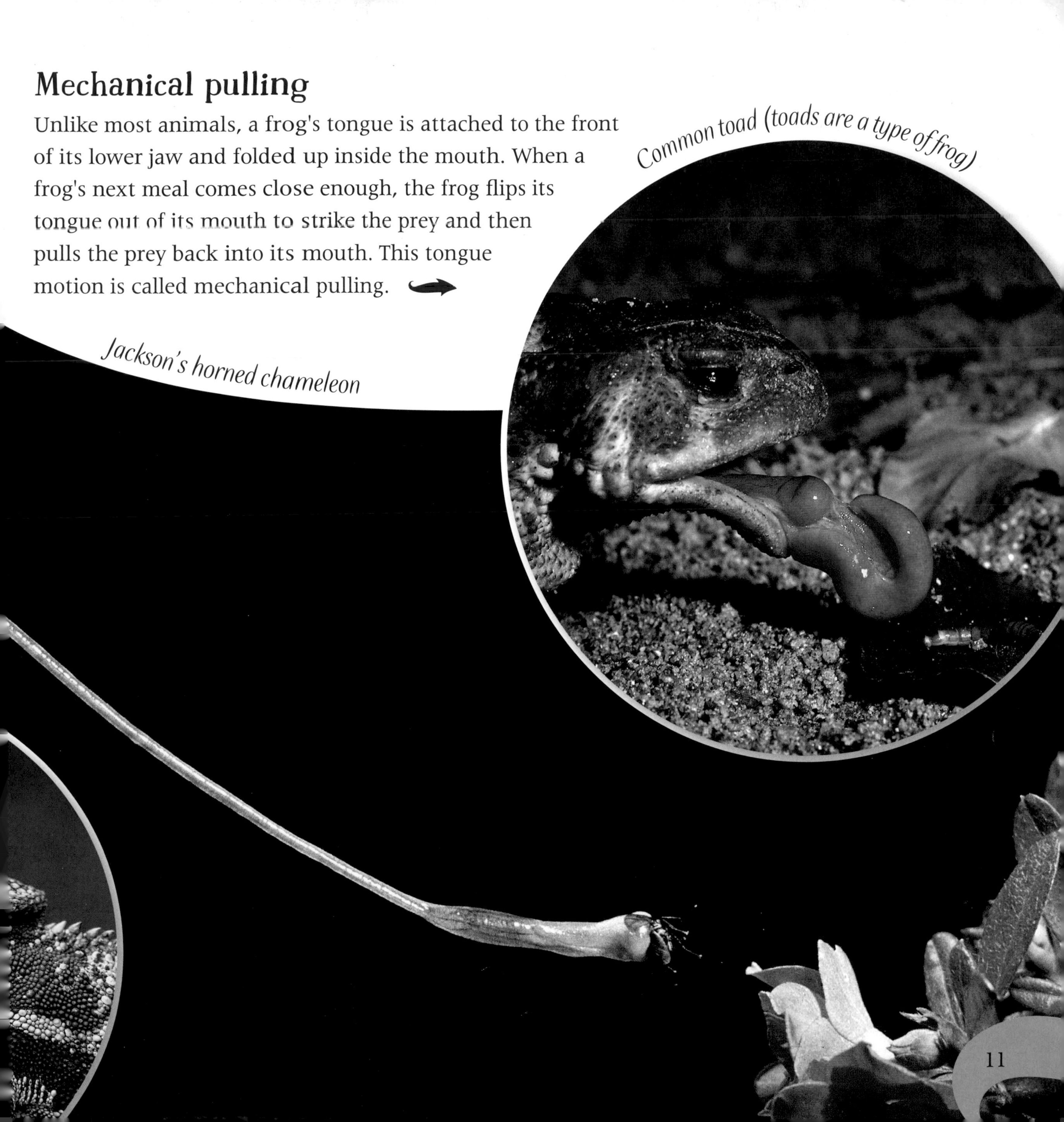

Common toad (toads are a type of frog)

Jackson's horned chameleon

Tongues for probing

Woodpeckers, such as this green woodpecker (right), feed on invertebrates and their larvae in tiny crevices in trees. They have a long, narrow tongue, which when extended is ideal for probing into the holes that their prey live in.

That's a wrap!

When a woodpecker isn't using its tongue, it is stored in a cavity inside the head that wraps around the brain!

The tongue is covered in sticky saliva and the tip has backwards-pointing barbs. It's all perfectly designed to snare unlucky invertebrates.

Woodpecker tongue

Fast food

Hummingbirds are amazing flying machines – they can even fly backwards! They need the energy from sugar-rich nectar to keep their wings flapping up to 100 times per second. When feeding, a hummingbird doesn't need to perch – it hovers, inserts its long beak into the flower and probes its even longer tongue into the flower's nectar. The hummingbird then pulls its tongue back into the beak again, 10 times a second or more.

Green-crowned brilliant hummingbird

Forked tongue

The tip of a hummingbird's tongue 'unzips' into a forked shape that pumps the sugary liquid nectar up along two tiny grooves

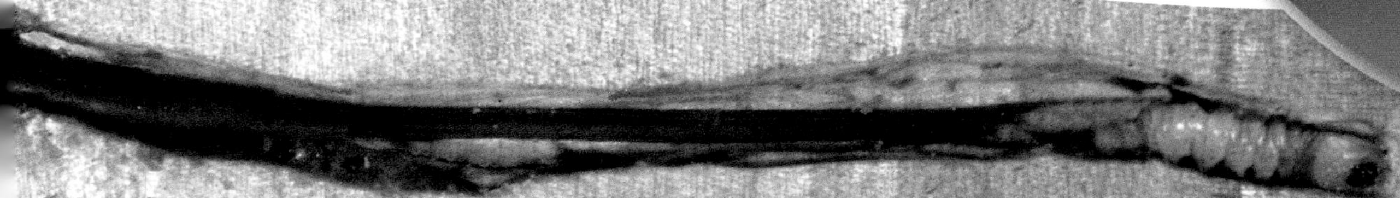

Orange nectar bat

Several species of bat feed on nectar. Some have a hairy tongue that mops up the liquid, others have grooves on the tongue that the nectar runs through.

Tongues for fishing

A Bryde's* whale is a type of baleen whale. The biggest of the baleen whales – the blue whale – is the largest animal known to have lived and can grow up to 30 metres long. Bryde's whales are smaller at about 15 metres long.

Most of their diet is made up of tiny crustaceans called krill, which are just 1–2 centimetres long. Baleen whales use their large tongue to help trap and then swallow their food.

This Bryde's whale has taken a large mouthful of seawater and krill.

Krill

* Bryde's is pronounced '*Broo-dess*'.

Keratin

Humpback whale

Keratin

Baleen plates are made from keratin, the same substance that is found in fingernails, claws and fur. A Bryde's whale has between 250–400 baleen plates.

Snap and trap

When it is feeding, a baleen whale opens its mouth and lunges forwards. Its mouth fills with water that contains thousands of krill. The whale then shuts its mouth and pushes its tongue forwards to force the water out through baleen plates that hang from its upper jaw. The krill are trapped by the baleen plates and are then swallowed. In a single day, a blue whale can eat up to 40 million krill, which altogether weigh more than 3 tonnes.

A humpback whale uses its tongue and baleen plates to filter fish from water, in much the same way as a Bryde's whale filters krill.

Tongues for filtering

With their spindly legs, long neck and pink feathers, flamingoes are remarkable-looking birds. When feeding, they sift through water in search of brine shrimp and algae. They swish their beak upside down in shallow water, from side to side.

As they do this, their large tongue moves quickly backwards and forwards. This action draws water, shrimp and algae into the beak and then pushes the water out. The food is caught on rows of bristles on the tongue and on the inside of the beak.

A flamingo's flat-fronted beak is designed to lie perfectly on the bed of a lake.

Lesser flamingo

The curved bristles on a flamingo's tongue point backwards to help this bird trap its food.

Lamellae

The shoveler duck has more than 100 fine comb-like projections, or lamellae, along the sides of its shovel-shaped beak. These act like a sieve when the bird draws water into its mouth. As the tongue pushes against the lamellae water escapes, but tiny aquatic creatures and seeds are caught by them – and the duck swallows them.

Canada geese have tiny keratin 'teeth' running along each side of their tongue to help them filter out food from the water.

Deadly tongues

Some animals use their tongue to confuse other animals – which they then eat! This is called 'lingual luring', and the world's best are alligator snapping turtles.

These reptiles have a worm-like blob at the end of their tongue. They rest motionless on the bottom of a swamp, with their mouth held open. They wiggle their tongue and wait for a fish to swim into their mouth to feed on the 'worm'. Then, *snap!* The turtle has its next meal.

A fish swims dangerously close to an alligator snapping turtle's jaws as it investigates what looks like a tasty worm.

Cute but deadly

Slow lorises might look cute, but these primates have poisonous saliva and glands under their armpits that produce toxic chemicals. If threatened by a snake, a loris will lick its armpit to pick up the venom on its tongue. The toxic chemicals mix with the loris's poisonous saliva, so when it bites the snake it delivers a double-deadly dose of venom.

Ripple effects

The snowy egret flicks its tongue rapidly on the surface of water. The ripples attract small fish, which the hungry egret grabs.

Tongues that pull

Tigers are fearsome predators. They ambush and kill large animals, including deer, buffalo and goats. Tigers eat the flesh of their prey, but they can't digest the fur.

This isn't a problem, though, because a tiger's tongue is rougher than sandpaper. When a tiger draws its tongue over a dead animal, it strips off the fur and skin, allowing the big cat to eat the meat underneath.

Bengal tiger

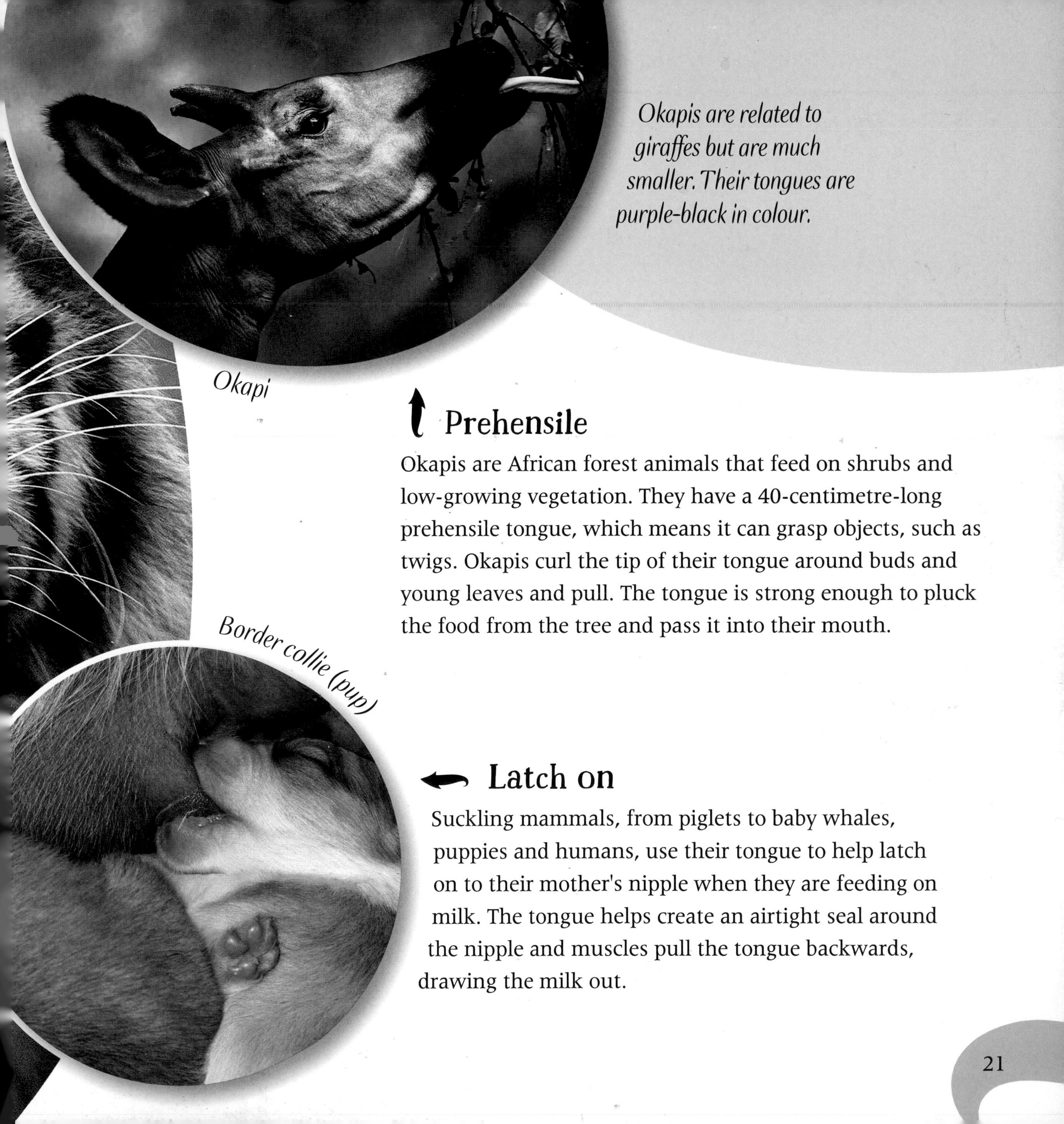

Okapis are related to giraffes but are much smaller. Their tongues are purple-black in colour.

Okapi

Prehensile

Okapis are African forest animals that feed on shrubs and low-growing vegetation. They have a 40-centimetre-long prehensile tongue, which means it can grasp objects, such as twigs. Okapis curl the tip of their tongue around buds and young leaves and pull. The tongue is strong enough to pluck the food from the tree and pass it into their mouth.

Border collie (pup)

Latch on

Suckling mammals, from piglets to baby whales, puppies and humans, use their tongue to help latch on to their mother's nipple when they are feeding on milk. The tongue helps create an airtight seal around the nipple and muscles pull the tongue backwards, drawing the milk out.

Tongues that grip

Penguins hunt fish and squid underwater. They swallow their prey alive – so it will still be wriggling as it tries to get away. Fortunately for the penguins, the top of their tongue is covered with many sharp little papillae, each one pointing backwards. These may be up to 1 centimetre long. The papillae help the penguin grasp slippery items of prey and shovel them down its throat.

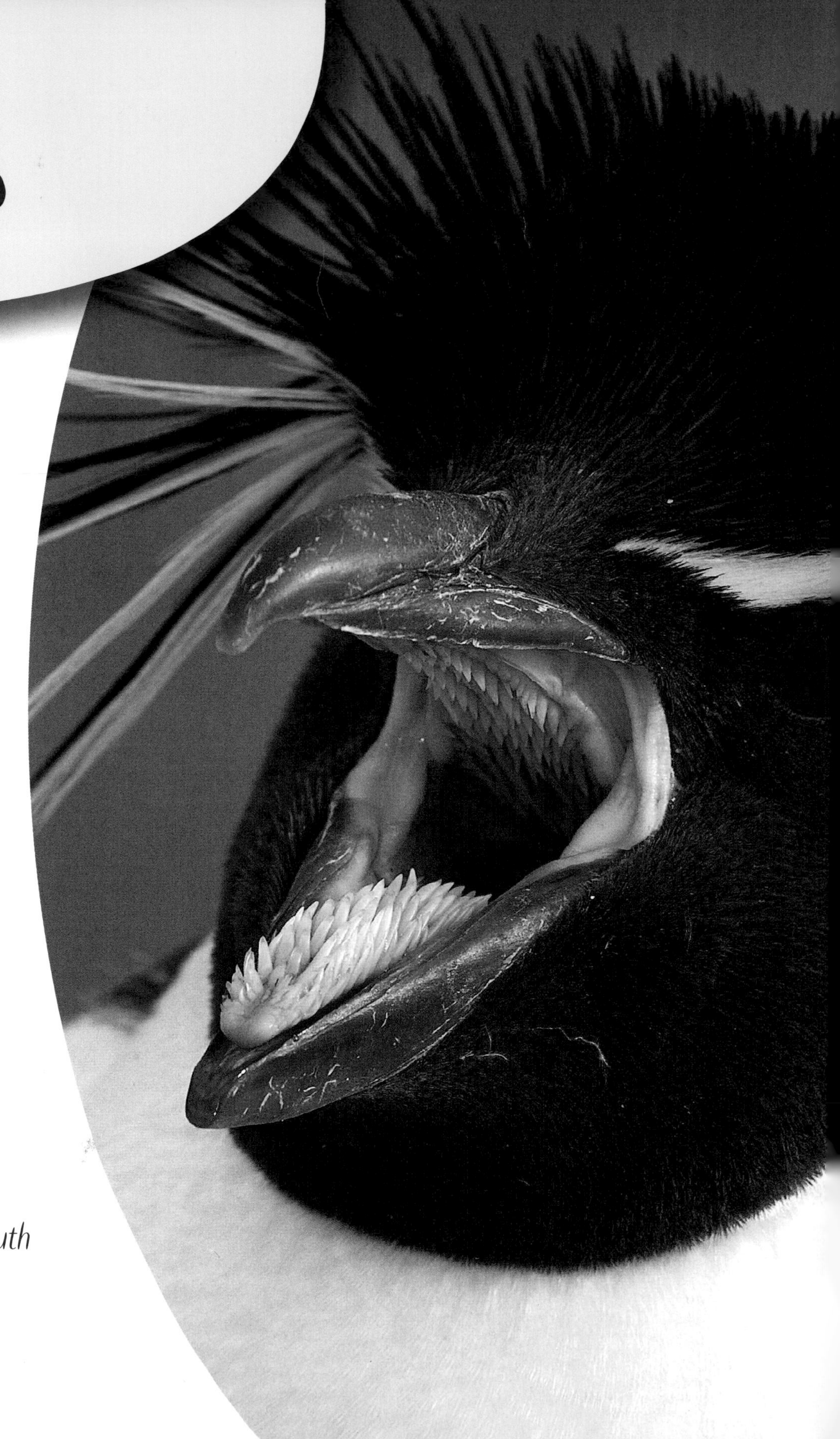

Rockhopper penguins are small but very loud. The rows of papillae on this penguin's tongue and the roof of its mouth are clear to see as it calls.

Atlantic puffin

Common kingfisher

What a mouthful!

When it has hungry chicks to feed, an Atlantic puffin needs to supply them with as much food as possible. That means cramming dozens of sand eels into its beak. A rough tongue and sharp barbs on the roof of its mouth keep the fish from slithering out of its mouth as it returns to the nest burrow from a fishing expedition.

Atlantic puffin (and sand eels)

The kingfisher is another fishing bird. It also has papillae on its tongue to make sure its catch doesn't get away!

Tongues for tasting

Many animals have taste buds on their tongue. Rabbits have several thousand of these microscopic mushroom- and leaf-shaped lobes, so they have a great sense of taste. Just like humans, they can detect bitter, sweet, salty and sour flavours. They can also work out which plants are safe to eat and which are toxic – a very important skill for an animal that eats nothing *but* plants!

Rabbits, like this lop-eared domestic rabbit, have a pink tongue, just like humans do.

Domestic pig

Good taste

No one knows what it's like to be another animal, so no one can be sure what food tastes like to other animals. However, scientists *do* know that a pig has about 17,000 taste buds on its tongue – nearly twice as many as on a human tongue – so a pig probably has a very good sense of taste indeed.

Redtail catfish

Swimming tongues

No animal has a better sense of taste than a catfish. These fish live in murky, muddy water and have been called 'swimming tongues' because they have up to 175,000 taste buds – 10 times as many as a pig. These are not just on their tongue, though, but all over their body, which means they 'taste' the water they swim through as they search for food.

Tongues for finding prey

Dragons are not just for fairy tales. The Komodo dragon is very real and is one of the most fearsome animals on Earth. This tropical reptile grows up to 3 metres long and can kill pigs, deer and even humans, as well as feeding on dead animals.

It has a long, deeply forked tongue, which it flicks out of its mouth to 'taste' the air to detect rotting dead animals up to 9 kilometres away. By moving its head and tongue from side to side, the animal can work out which direction to walk in to track down its next meal.

Wild goats are a favourite food of Komodo dragons.

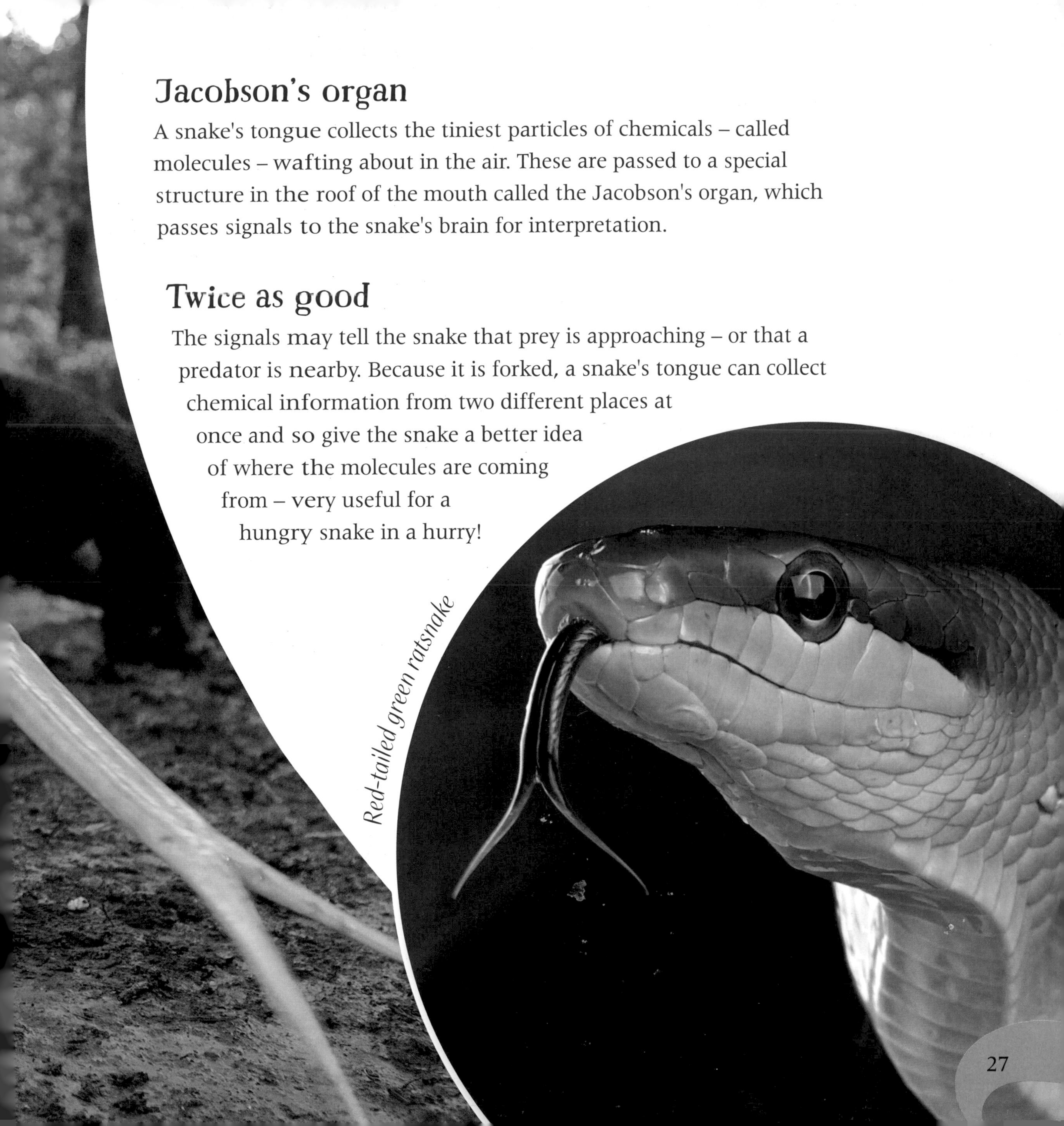

Jacobson's organ

A snake's tongue collects the tiniest particles of chemicals – called molecules – wafting about in the air. These are passed to a special structure in the roof of the mouth called the Jacobson's organ, which passes signals to the snake's brain for interpretation.

Twice as good

The signals may tell the snake that prey is approaching – or that a predator is nearby. Because it is forked, a snake's tongue can collect chemical information from two different places at once and so give the snake a better idea of where the molecules are coming from – very useful for a hungry snake in a hurry!

Red-tailed green ratsnake

Tongues for cleaning

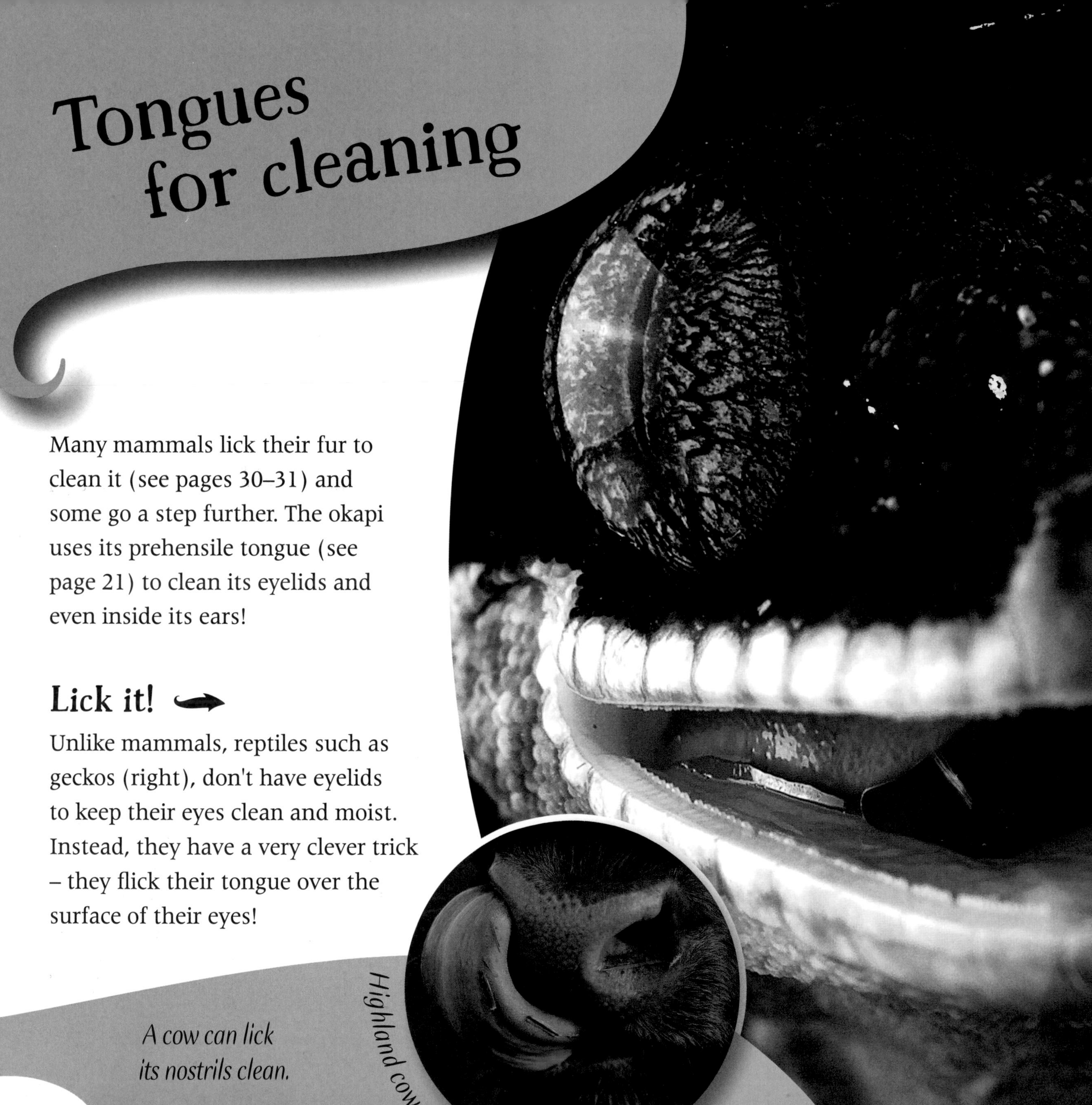

Many mammals lick their fur to clean it (see pages 30–31) and some go a step further. The okapi uses its prehensile tongue (see page 21) to clean its eyelids and even inside its ears!

Lick it!

Unlike mammals, reptiles such as geckos (right), don't have eyelids to keep their eyes clean and moist. Instead, they have a very clever trick – they flick their tongue over the surface of their eyes!

Highland cow

A cow can lick its nostrils clean.

Banded gecko

Bulldog

Thomson's gazelle

Baby bath ↑

After they've given birth, many mammal mothers lick their newborn offspring. As well as cleaning their babies, this also stimulates their breathing.

↓ Fighting infection

If a dog is wounded it will lick the cut. Saliva on the dog's tongue contains chemicals that help stop the bleeding and fight disease-spreading bacteria. Other animals do this, too, including cats, horses, mice and primates.

Tongues for grooming

Cats are super-fussy cleaners. From large lions and tigers to small bobcats and domestic cats, they love to groom themselves – licking their fur to remove loose fur, dirt and fleas. Domestic cats spend at least a quarter of their waking hours licking themselves. If you've ever been licked by one, you will know that a cat's tongue is very rough. That's because it is covered in hundreds of tiny, backward-curved papillae.

Lions (and some other animals, such as dogs) show affection to each other and strengthen social bonds by grooming one another.

Keep cool

The tips of a cat's papillae are hollow and pick up saliva from inside the cat's mouth. When it grooms its fur, the saliva washes it clean and cools the skin at the same time. Over the course of a day, a domestic cat will transfer about 50 millilitres of saliva to its fur – that's the equivalent of a fifth of a cup of water.

Domestic cat (kitten)

Close-up of a domestic cat's papillae

A cat's tongue is like a very smart comb. If it was smooth, it wouldn't make such a good cleaning apparatus.

Terrifying tongues

Blue-tongued skinks, or 'blueys', are reptiles that live in dry areas of Australia and Indonesia. They are active during the day, searching on the ground for insects, spiders and snails. Skinks are vulnerable to attack by predators, such as snakes and birds of prey.

Blueys are not naturally aggressive animals, but if threatened they have an unusual defence – they hiss and stick out their large, bright blue tongue to startle aggressors! The shocked predator may hesitate just long enough to give the skink time to make its escape.

Dazzled

The more it feels threatened, the more of its tongue a skink reveals. Zoologists have discovered that the back of the tongue – the last part that the skink shows – reflects more ultraviolet (UV) light. Animals that are sensitive to UV rays, such as birds of prey, may be dazzled by its brightness.

Cooling tongues

Have you ever watched a dog chasing a ball or playing with another dog? Often, after it's been racing around a lot, it will stop and then start panting, with its mouth open and its tongue hanging out as far as it will go.

When a dog overheats, this is one way it can become more comfortable. Saliva on its tongue evaporates more quickly with the mouth open, cooling the surface of its tongue and the blood vessels within it. Gradually, the dog's temperature drops and it can start playing again.

A Great Dane's tongue hangs out of its mouth as it pants to cool down.

Heat loss

Unlike mammals, which can sweat to lose heat when they're very hot, birds don't have sweat glands, so they keep cool by opening their beak and panting. As they breathe quickly, heat moves out of their body and the bare skin of the tongue and the inside of the mouth loses heat. Watch birds on a very hot day and you might see them doing this.

Cape glossy starling

Common iguana

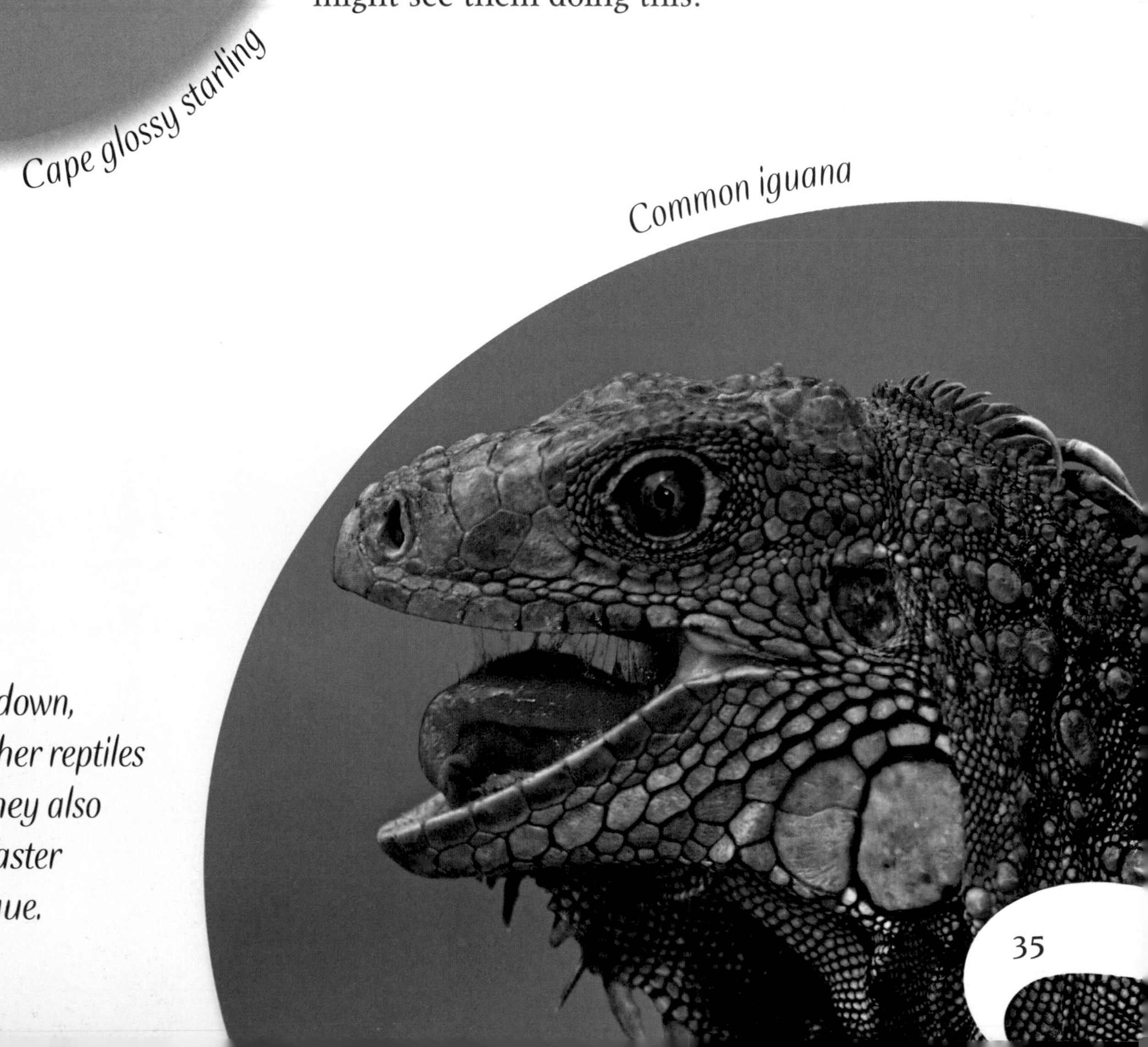

When they need to cool down, iguanas, crocodiles and other reptiles will move into the shade. They also open their mouth to allow faster evaporation from their tongue.

Tongues for speaking

When we speak, sound waves are produced by our larynx, or voice box. We form different letter sounds by changing the position and shape of our jaw, lips and tongue.

For example: to make the sound of the 'i' in 'thing', the tongue has to be arched high in the mouth; for the 'a' in 'father' the tongue is flat in the bottom of the mouth; and to speak the 'l' in 'last', the tongue must touch the back of our upper teeth. Without a tongue, we could make lots of different noises, but we couldn't produce clear letter sounds.

This person is making an 'l' sound where the tongue touches the back of the upper teeth.

African grey parrot

Mimic

Parrots are well known for their ability to mimic (copy) human speech and African greys are probably the best. Scientists now know that they are able to make vowel sounds by moving the position of their muscular, nimble tongue. A tongue movement of just 1 millimetre makes a big difference to the sound coming out of this bird's mouth!

Common hill myna

In the wild, these clever birds don't mimic other birds or animals, but in captivity they will often mimic human speech.

Tongues for communicating

Black-and-white colobus monkeys (right) are leaf-eating primates of African forests. They communicate different messages by clicking the tongue from the roof to the floor of the mouth. If an unwelcome visitor approaches, a colobus will issue warnings, repeating loud single, double or triple tongue clicks. To convey a welcome to another monkey, it will click more softly.

Small primates called tamarins don't click their tongue – but they do flick it in and out of their mouth to indicate their mood.

Emperor tamarin

Lesser hedgehog tenrec

High-pitched squeaks

While they are feeding, hedgehog-like tenrecs in Madagascar stay in contact with each other by making squeaky tongue-clicks. Many of the sounds are so high-pitched they are beyond the range of normal human hearing and can only be heard by using a device called a bat-detector.

Egyptian rousette fruit bat

Echolocation

Some bats use their tongue to find out where prey is. Most bats navigate in the dark by making high-pitched squeals. These calls echo off trees, buildings and flying insects, so the bats can avoid collisions and track down their prey. This is called echolocation. Egyptian fruit bats also use echolocation, but rather than squealing they click their tongue and listen for the echo.

South American tapir

South American tapirs let each other know where they are in dense forest by clicking their tongues.

Fast, heavy and long tongues

Chameleons have possibly the fastest-accelerating tongues in the animal kingdom (see pages 10–11). Some can accelerate from 0 to 97 kph in around 0.001 seconds – faster than a fighter jet. Smaller chameleons, such as the rosette-nosed chameleon, are generally faster than larger chameleon species.

A Mediterranean chameleon (main photo), snares a grasshopper with its tongue.

The tiny but speedy rosette-nosed chameleon is only about 5 centimetres long.

Big and heavy

The prize for the world's biggest tongue goes to a whale. An adult blue whale's tongue weighs 2.7 tonnes – as heavy as a giraffe – and is 5 metres long when extended. When it takes a giant gulp (see pages 14–15), 90,000 litres of seawater floods into its mouth and it needs such a large tongue to push the weight of the water out through its baleen plates.

Blue whale

A sun bear can poke its 25-centimetre tongue far into a beehive to extract honey and bee larvae.

Malayan sun bear

Even longer tongues!

The Morgan's sphinx moth (right) lives on the African island of Madagascar. Its body is 7 centimetres long, but its proboscis unrolls to three times that distance. It needs to be this long to reach nectar inside trumpet-shaped flowers.

Spur

The Darwin's orchid has a very long spur with nectar in the bottom of it. Only an animal with a long proboscis, such as the Morgan's sphinx moth, can reach the nectar inside.

Darwin's orchid

Lap it up

Pangolins are nocturnal animals that live in tropical Africa and Asia. They are covered in scales, not fur, and feed mostly on ants and termites, which they find with their amazing sense of smell. Lacking teeth, they lap up their prey (and water) with a long, thin, sticky tongue that is as long as the animal's body – 40 centimetres.

Sunda pangolin

Flower powered

A tube-lipped nectar bat's tongue is 8.5 centimetres long. This may not sound particularly long, but the bat is only the size of a mouse, so its tongue is one-and-a-half times its body length! The bat needs such a long tongue to reach nectar deep within flowers.

Tube-lipped nectar bat

Where does this bat keep its tongue when its not sipping nectar? It extends down into the animal's chest, between its heart and breastbone!

Weird tongues

A giraffe has a purple or blackish tongue due to the density of melanin (dark colour pigments) in it. No one really knows why this is so, but many scientists believe that the melanin provides extra protection from ultraviolet radiation in strong African sunshine. This keeps their delicate tongues from getting sunburnt as the animals pluck leaves high in trees.

A giraffe's favourite foods are leaves and twigs, but the plants they eat are often covered in sharp thorns. To protect against prickles, a giraffe has a tongue that is very tough. It's also long enough to lick its own nostrils clean!

Tongue or brush?

Lorikeets are parrots with very fine tufts at the end of their tongue. It looks like a tiny brush. The tufts, which have earned the birds the name 'brush-tongued parrots', help them pick up pollen and water.

Rainbow lorikeet

Two tongues

Some primates, such as slow lorises, have two tongues! The second tongue is underneath the main tongue and has a brush-like appearance. It is used to remove hair from a specialised set of teeth called a toothcomb, which the animal uses to groom its fur.

Slow loris

Useless tongues!

Frogs in the family Pipidae are called 'tongueless' frogs. They do actually have a tongue, but it is attached to the floor of the mouth and can't be moved, so the tongue is useless in helping these frogs to eat. Instead, tongueless frogs use their front limbs when they are feeding.

African clawed frog

Activities to try

Long tongues

The tongue of a tube-lipped nectar bat is 1.5 times longer than its body. If you were this bat, how long would your tongue be? If you had the tongue of a chameleon, how long would it be? How about the tongue of a giant anteater, or the proboscis of a Morgan's sphinx moth?

Tongue-clicking language

Design a tongue-clicking code language. You could use a mixture of quick clicks, slow clicks, high-pitched clicks from the front of the mouth and deeper clicks from the back of the mouth to represent letters or words. See if you can get friends to work out what you're 'saying'.

Tongue-tied

Slowly speak aloud each letter of the alphabet, from A to Z. Concentrate on the position of your tongue for each letter. Does the tip of your tongue move as you work through the alphabet? Get a friend to help you note the tongue's position each time.

Glossary

algae very small plant-like living things
ambush surprise attack
aquatic living in or near water
bacteria single-celled micro-organism; many can cause diseases, such as salmonella
cavity a hole, such as in a tree
crevice a small crack or hole
crustacean animal with a hard shell and no backbone, such as a lobster, shrimp or crab
density the amount of something in a given area
evaporate when water turns to water vapour
hover to stay in one place in the air
invertebrate animal without a backbone; snails, crustaceans, spiders, jellyfish and insects are all invertebrates
larva (plural: larvae) the immature (young) form of an insect, such as a caterpillar or maggot
lingual relating to the tongue
lobe a round, flat body part
mammal warm-blooded animal with hair or fur that drinks its mother's milk when young
melanin dark brown or black pigment found in skin
nectar sugary liquid found in flowers that attracts nectar-drinking animals in order to aid with pollination
nimble quick and light movements or actions
organ part of the body that has an essential function, such as the heart or brain
particle minute piece of matter
pigment naturally occuring colours, such as those found in skin, eyes or fur
pollen tiny grains found in flowers that fertilise the female part of a flower
predator animal that hunts and eats other animals
prehensile tongue or tail that is flexible and able to hold objects
prey animal that is eaten by other animals
primates mammal such as a human, monkey, lemur, ape or loris
probe to explore something, such as a hole or crevice
reptile cold-blooded animal with dry scaly skin
saliva liquid made in the mouth that helps with swallowing and digesting food
sift remove bits of food from another substance, such as water or mud
spur a tube that grows from the base of a flower
toxic poisonous
tropical relating to the tropics – the areas above and below the equator
ultraviolet light waves that are close to the violet end of the visible spectrum, but are invisible to humans
venom poisonous liquid made by animals, such as spiders
zoologist animal scientist

Further information

Books

Animal Superheroes by Raphaël Martin (Wayland, 2016)

Animal Tails by Tim Harris (Wayland, 2019)

The Poo That Animals Do by Paul Mason and illustrated by Tony De Saulles (Wayland, 2018)

The Wee That Animals Pee by Paul Mason and illustrated by Tony De Saulles (Wayland, 2019)

Wildlife Worlds (series) by Tim Harris (Franklin Watts, 2019)

Index